Who Wants This Puppy?

Story by
Pat Ternovetsky

Illustrations by
Zane Belton

Peanut Butter Press

Have you ever wondered what it's like to be a puppy?

It can be fun and exciting and scary and lots of things.

Let me tell you my story.

I was born on a farm with my eight brothers and sisters. We lived together with our mother in a warm pen full of straw. We played and ate during the day and we snuggled up at night. What a great start to life!

How lucky I felt when a man and lady came to the farm and picked me to be a Christmas present for their children! They put me in a big box beside the tree so their son and daughter could find me on Christmas morning. When the children saw me, they jumped up and down with excitement!

4

All the holiday guests loved me and I thought living with this family was going to be fun!

At first, the children played with me **a lot**.

But then January came and everyone in the family got busy. They went to work and to school . . . leaving me **all** by myself **all** day long.

When I was alone, I got tired of waiting and I decided to have some fun. Those shoes in the closet looked so tasty and smelled so good that I just had to give them a chew!

I liked to topple the shiny can in the bathroom and spread the fluffy white paper all over. Sometimes I forgot where to "go" and left wet spots on the floor!

When spring came, my family tied me up in the yard.

What was under that lovely green grass? I dug holes to try to find out.

What kept moving behind the fence? I barked to try to scare it away.

Where was everybody out there going? I chewed through my rope to get away and follow them.

One day, I heard the dad say, "This dog is too much trouble. We don't have time to take care of him and clean up his messes. **We'll have to get rid of him!**"

Was I really that much trouble?
Who would ever want me?

My family took me to a **strange** place. I ended up in a cage all by myself. There were lots of other dogs around me and so much barking that my ears hurt!

Someone brought me food, but I didn't feel like eating. I was so lonely that I just sat and cried.

After a while, I was given my own room. There was a big window, a comfortable bed, and a toy bone for me to chew on . . . but I still wasn't happy. It wasn't like a real home.

A kind lady came and spoke very nicely to me. She took me outside for a walk and some playtime, but I was still sad.

The next morning, I noticed a family peeking through the glass. Were they looking for a puppy to take home? I hoped so! I scampered over to the window and put my paws up on the ledge. The boy in the family looked right at me and smiled. I started to feel better and my tail began to wag.

MAX

"Hey, Mom and Dad, why don't we get **this** little puppy?" the boy asked hopefully. "The sign says his name is Max. He looks really smart. I think Haley would like him too."

"Yes, Noah," the mother agreed. "I think he might be a good dog for our family. He isn't too big, and he seems to like us."

The father added, "Let's talk to one of the workers and find out more about this little fellow and whether he would be the right pet for us."

Yip!

Noah's family gave me a collar and a leash and took me home in their car that very day! When I got in the car, I cried because I was so nervous. Noah brought me closer to him and made sure I felt more comfortable.

On the first night at my new home, I was so excited that I made a **big** wet spot on the floor. I hid under the table. **Would my family be mad at me?**

They weren't mad.
The mom cleaned
up the wet spot and
Noah reminded me
about where I was
supposed to "go."

When I went outside to play the next day, I smelled something **wonderful** under the apple tree. I got really muddy when I tried to find out what was hidden there.

My family didn't yell. Instead, Noah took me inside and gave me a bath.

It's great living here! Noah and his family give me lots of attention. They say having a dog is a big responsibility, and they know they have to have patience at first.

My family still needs to remind me about where to "go," but I'm getting better at remembering.

My family makes sure my water dish is always full. They give me healthy food to eat . . . and sometimes I get **treats!** They remember to groom my coat. I don't mind having my teeth brushed because they use toothpaste that tastes like chicken.

CHICKEN

I'll never forget the first time I had
my nails **clipped!**

Every week, I go to a school with other dogs where I'm learning to sit, stay, and lay down when my family gives a command. I'm also learning to come when they call my name, but that's harder for me . . . because sometimes I get busy doing something and I don't hear them!

It's Noah's job to take me for a long walk every day so I can get my exercise. He's training me to walk on his left side so I won't get tangled up in the leash.

I'm trying not to pull too hard because I don't want to hurt Noah's arm.

Whenever my family has to go out and leave me alone, they make sure I'm in my kennel. That way, I can't get into trouble in the house. Inside my kennel, there's a fluffy blanket and lots of toys. This is my little home and I like being in there. Besides, my family never leaves me alone for very long.

Noah gives me lots of love and says I'm the best dog in the whole world! I'm very lucky that he wanted **this** puppy!

To Murray, Michael, Julie, and Bob, my biggest fans,
and to Noah and Haley, my favourite little people!
- P. T.

Dedicated to Mickey Mouse and his creator, Walt Disney.
- Z. B.

Text copyright © 2008 by Pat Ternovetsky
Illustrations copyright © 2008 by Zane Belton

Peanut Butter Press
#9-1060 Dakota Street, Winnipeg, MB, R2N 1P2
www.peanutbutterpress.ca

Designed by Lee Huscroft
Edited by Mark d'Almeida

Printed and bound in Canada by Friesens

Library and Archives Canada Cataloguing in Publication

Ternovetsky, Pat, 1954-
    Who wants this puppy? / Pat Ternovetsky ; Zane Belton, illustrator.

ISBN 978-0-9735579-6-1

    I. Belton, Zane, 1999- II. Title.
PS8639.E74W46 2008   jC813'.6   C2008-901588-6

If you are having trouble training your dog, contact your local animal shelter for advice.

Part of the proceeds from the sale of this book will go to support animal shelters across Canada.